# WHAT IS A WHISPERY SECRET?

# WHAT IS A
# WHISPERY SECRET?

By Lois Hobart      Pictures by Martha Alexander

Parents' Magazine Press • New York

*E*

*By the Same Author:*

MEXICAN MURAL
PATRIOT'S LADY
STRANGERS AMONG US
BEHIND THE WALLS
LAURIE, PHYSICAL THERAPIST
ELAINE FORREST, VISITING NURSE
A PALETTE FOR INGRID
KATIE AND HER CAMERA

*For Tony . . . may the promise of his youth be realized in the years to come*

What is a whisper?

It's a tiny little quiet little
soft little voice—

*like this.*

Can you whisper?

In a tiny little quiet little
soft little voice—*like this?*

Who whispers?

The grass whispers when it's long and rustly.

The leaves on the trees
whisper in the breeze.

And they whisper again in the fall,
as they float to the ground
in crisp curls of yellow, red or brown.

A kitten whispers when it leaps into your lap—

to burrow itself into a warm cuddly
cosy ball, while you stroke its
furry satin back.

What is a secret?

It's something nobody knows but you—
or nobody in the world but you and me.
That's your secret.

The secret may be that you are not
a little boy or girl at all.
But a pony galloping over the hill.

Or a daddy building bookshelves
in the basement.

It may be something to see or hear.
Like the cubbyhole in the kitchen.

Or a bullfrog puffing out his throat
in the pond.

Then what is a *whispery* secret?

It's a very special secret.
That is told in a tiny little
quiet little soft little voice—
*like this.*

Have you ever seen a mare look around
and nuzzle her colt?


She's telling a whispery secret.

Have you ever seen a giraffe stretch
her winding neck way down to lick her
spindly-legged spotted baby?

Or two squirrels squatting on their haunches,
bright-eyed, flicking their tails
and nibbling nuts?
They're all telling whispery secrets!

Would you like to hear
the whisperiest secret of all?

Then put your arms around my neck,
and your cheek right next to mine . . .
And I'll tell you something that
nobody else knows,

in a tiny little quiet little
soft little voice—*like this . . .*

The whisperiest secret of all is — *I love you!*

## ABOUT THE AUTHOR

Lois Hobart (Mrs. Harold Black) is the author of many books for both children and young adults. She makes her home in San Miguel de Allende, Mexico where she and her husband have founded a world-famous riding school as well as an equestrian shop and an art gallery. Mrs. Black was born in Minneapolis and is a graduate of the University of Minnesota. She is the mother of a teen-age son, Tony, and in addition to writing, works as a free-lance photographer.

## ABOUT THE ARTIST

Martha Alexander illustrates regularly for a number of nationally distributed magazines. Her gentle and sensitive art work can also be seen in *Grandfathers Are to Love* and *Grandmothers Are to Love,* recently published by Parents' Magazine Press. Mrs. Alexander was born in Augusta, Georgia. She studied at the Cincinnati Art Academy and at the University of Hawaii. She now lives and works in New York City.